SECRETS OF THE LIBRARY OF DOOM

DEAD LETTERS

BY MICHAEL DAHL
ILLUSTRATED BY PATRICIO CLAREY

STONE ARCH BOOKS
a capstone imprint

Secrets of the Library of Doom is published by
Stone Arch Books, an imprint of Capstone.
1710 Roe Crest Drive
North Mankato, Minnesota 56003
www.capstonepub.com

Library of Congress Cataloging-in-Publication Data is
available on the Library of Congress website.

ISBN: 978-1-4965-9723-6 (hardcover)
ISBN: 978-1-4965-9897-4 (paperback)
ISBN: 978-1-4965-9742-7 (ebook PDF)

Summary: Evil silent letters, like the W of *swords* and the K
of *knives*, rest in the Graveyard of Dead Letters. When the
wicked wizard Spellbinder uses their power to create a fierce
weapon, even the mighty Librarian will struggle to defeat it.

Designed by Hilary Wacholz

Printed and bound in the USA.
PA117

TABLE OF CONTENTS

The Library of Doom is a hidden fortress.
It holds the world's largest collection
of strange and dangerous books.

Behold the Librarian. He defends the Library—and
the world—from super-villains, clever thieves,
and fierce monsters. Many of his adventures
have remained secret. Now they can be told.

SECRET #2,003
SILENCE IS A POWERFUL WEAPON.

Chapter One

SILENT TOMBS

No creatures howl. No insects **BUZZ**. No winds sigh.

Only shadows **STIR** in the silent graveyard.

One shadow moves quickly between the **STONE** buildings.

The **SHADOW** belongs to a man.

His heavy boots **CRUNCH** on the stone path.

His dark coat rustles as it **SWIRLS** behind him.

It is the LIBRARIAN. He is hunting in the Graveyard of Dead Letters.

The Librarian passes by the tomb of the Dead G.

He *GLIDES* by the tomb of the Dead H.

In the graveyard lie all the dead and silent letters. They are found in words, but they make no sound.

Like the K in *knife* or the W in *sword*.

The Librarian walks past more **DARK** buildings. Then he hears a voice behind a wall.

That's him! thinks the Librarian.

Chapter Two

WIZARD'S SUIT OF ARMOR

The Librarian **FLIES** to the top of the wall.

He sees an old foe waiting for him on the other side.

"SPELLBINDER! What did you do with my Aide?" asks the Librarian.

The **WIZARD** laughs. "Your Aide has been quite helpful to me," he says.

The Spellbinder waves to a suit of armor standing behind him. "What do you think of my new creation?" he asks.

The *GIANT* armor is covered with letters—dead letters.

It holds a long **SWORD** by its side.

"You didn't tell me where my Aide is," the Librarian says.

"Oh, but I did," says the Spellbinder.

GGRRRRNNNNN!

The suit of armor creaks. Its helmet **TURNS** toward the Librarian.

The hero sees a face in the helmet. His Aide is TRAPPED inside.

Chapter Three

LIVING WEAPON

"Your friend adds life to my spell," says the Spellbinder. "He is trapped in my armor made of silent letters. They are the most powerful letters in the world."

The Spellbinder **THROWS** his hat at the armor.

He shouts, "The silent letter E can turn a *hat* into *hate*!"

The wizard's hat BURSTS into sparks of fire.

The fire spreads across the armor.
Then the armor raises its sword.

The Librarian raises his hands. RAYS of light shoot out from his fingers.

AAAEEEEEHHHHHHHH! screams a voice inside the armor.

"If you **DESTROY** my armor," warns the Spellbinder, "you will also destroy your friend!"

I dare not hurt my Aide! thinks the Librarian. *But how can I remove him from that armor?*

The Librarian runs from the GIANT warrior.

He **LEAPS** over the stone walls.

KRROOOOM!

The armor smashes through the stone.

Nothing STOPS it.

"Silent letters are powerful!" shouts the Spellbinder. "You, Librarian, possess no silent letters. But your Aide has two!"

The armor *RUSHES* toward the Librarian.

Chapter Four

ENDLESS BRIDGE

The hero doesn't want to ATTACK his friend. The Librarian steps back.

He feels a powerful **WIND** behind him. He turns and sees an ancient bridge.

The bridge stretches over a bottomless pit of darkness. It is the Bridge of Silence.

HUGE statues of iron and stone line the bridge's sides. The Spellbinder laughs as he walks toward the Librarian.

"Many warriors come to a **TERRIBLE** end on this bridge," he says. "You will be next, Librarian!"

CLAANNNGGGG!

The armor smacks its sword against the bridge's statues.

The statues begin to MOVE. They climb off their platforms.

The statues **HURL** iron spears at the Librarian. The spears all have silent A's.

The Librarian holds up his hand. He **STOPS** the spears with an invisible wall of power.

More statues close in behind the Librarian.

The hero is **TRAPPED**.

Chapter Five

V IS FOR . . .

I can't fly away, thinks the Librarian.
I can't leave my Aide!

Suddenly the Librarian hears a whisper.

It comes from **DEEP** within the armor.

"The pit is very vast. It is very, very deep," says the voice.

The Librarian sees his Aide's face within the GIANT helmet.

The young man's eyes are full of PAIN.

He fights the WIZARD'S spell in order to speak to the Librarian.

Of course! thinks the Librarian. *My Aide has found a way to save us both!*

The GIANT armor swings its sword at the Librarian's head.

Before the blade FALLS, the hero shouts,

"Victory!"

Then a new sound begins to fill the graveyard.

VVVV-VVVV-VVVVVV-VVVVVVV!

The bridge **VIBRATES**. The bridge's statues turn to vapor. The Spellbinder vanishes from view.

CRRRAAAACCKKKKK!

Cracks **SPLIT** down the metal suit
of armor. The armor falls apart.

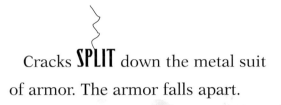

In the armor's place is a young man.

The Aide is freed from the **WIZARD'S** magic.

"You **HEARD** my voice," the Aide says, kneeling on the bridge.

"Yes," says the Librarian. "You made me remember that the letter V has a special power. It is the only letter that is *never* silent!"

The Librarian helps the Aide to his feet.

"Your **VALOR** and **VOCABULARY** has saved us both," the hero tells him.

They **WALK** off the empty bridge together, silently.

GLOSSARY

aide (AYD)—a helper

armor (AR-muhr)—clothing made of metal that protects the wearer from weapons

possess (puh-ZESS)—to own or to have

stir (STUR)—to make a small movement

tomb (TOOM)—a room or building where something dead is kept

valor (VA-lur)—bravery

vanish (VA-nish)—to pass from sight quickly and mysteriously

vapor (VAY-pur)—gas or steam

vast (VAST)—very large

vocabulary (voh-KAB-yuh-ler-ee)—all the words known and used by a person

warrior (WOR-ee-er)—a person who fights in battle and is known for having skill

wizard (WIZ-erd)—a person with magic powers

TALK ABOUT IT

1. The Librarian could have flown away from the fight, but he didn't. Why? What does this decision tell you about his character?

2. The author uses words to describe sounds in the story, like *KRROOOM* on page 21. Which spots do you think these words work well? Find spots where you think they could be added in or taken out.

WRITE ABOUT IT

1. This story takes place in a graveyard. Do you think it's a good setting? Why or why not? Write a paragraph arguing for your answer. Be sure to use examples from the story.

2. When the story starts, the Spellbinder has already captured the Aide. Write a story about how it happened, and be sure to make it exciting!

ABOUT THE AUTHOR

Michael Dahl is an award-winning author of more than 200 books for young people. He especially likes to write scary or weird fiction. His latest series are the sci-fi adventure Escape from Planet Alcatraz and School Bus of Horrors. As a child, Michael spent lots of time in libraries. "The creepier, the better," he says. These days, besides writing, he likes traveling and hunting for the one, true door that leads to the Library of Doom.

ABOUT THE ILLUSTRATOR

Patricio Clarey was born in 1978 in Argentina. He graduated in fine arts from the Martín A. Malharro School of Visual Arts, specializing in illustration and graphic design. Patricio currently lives in Barcelona, Spain, where he works as a freelance graphic designer and illustrator. He has created several comics and graphic novels, and his work has been featured in books and other publications.